The
Fox Hollow
Mystery

The
Fox Hollow
Mystery

BY

Mary Adrian

ILLUSTRATED BY

Lloyd Coe

WILDSIDE PRESS LLC

CONTENTS

The
Fox Hollow
Mystery

CHAPTER ONE

A Rabbit Disappears

It was the last day of school. Jeff opened his desk to make certain he had taken all his belongings. After stuffing a chewed-up pencil and an old eraser into his pocket, he closed the desk and said good-by to his teacher.

"Good-by, Jeffrey," she answered with an amused smile, since it was the third time he had made his farewell.

But Jeff was like that. He wanted to make sure he

had said good-by. With a satisfied grin he dashed out of the fourth-grade classroom like a squirrel on the run.

His classmates had left the building. Most of them were walking slowly in the direction of their homes, enjoying their freedom, while a few still remained in the playground. They were swinging on the bars like a pack of monkeys.

Jeff squinted through his heavy glasses, looked at the children, and then let his gaze travel over the rest of the playground.

"Gosh! Wouldn't you know it!" he said aloud to himself. "The kids in the Explorers Club have gone already, and I wanted to show them my agate. Gosh! That would happen to me."

A six-year-old boy stopped and stared at Jeff, puzzled. "Why are you talking to yourself?" he asked.

"Huh?" snorted Jeff, suddenly realizing that someone had spoken to him. "I wasn't talking to myself. I was thinking out loud."

"Well, then who are the Explorers?" asked the boy.

"Er . . . I can't tell you now." Jeff's voice sounded impatient, and he left the boy glaring after him as he raced out of the playground.

When he reached the road, a trailer truck was going by, filling the air with dust. Jeff coughed and sneezed, but as soon as the dust lifted, he hurried on his way to a wide-open field. It was not the usual route he took to walk home, for he was not going home. He wanted to catch up with the Explorers, especially if they were heading for the hut, a take-off station for their next expedition.

Jeff's guess was right. No sooner had his long legs reached the end of the field than he saw the Explorers, four in number, three boys and a girl. They were chasing one another around trees along a narrow road.

Suddenly they stopped their play and came together with heads almost bumping into one another. They began talking in low voices and acting so secretive that Jeff ran faster. When he reached the group, he stumbled over a rock in the road and landed flat at their feet in the dirt.

Theresa, who was called Toni because she played with boys, was the first to see him.

"Goodness! Are you hurt?" she asked anxiously, trying to help Jeff get up.

The boy rolled over on his back, blinked his eyes through his heavy glasses, and groaned. He was looking into four faces, each one showing concern, which was the last thing he wished to have happen, since he wanted to make a good impression on the Explorers.

Embarrassed and annoyed at his awkwardness, he slowly got to his feet. In silence he brushed the dirt from his pants.

"Are you sure you're all right?" asked Dick. He was president of the Explorers Club.

Jeff nodded and tried to smile, but the smile would not come, and he felt like running away and hiding. Then, remembering the agate in his pocket, he pulled it out and in a shy voice said, "I found this at Fox Hollow. I'm sure it's a prize agate. I don't think there is another stone like it in Oregon."

The four Explorers looked at the agate and then turned away, bored. It was the second time that Jeff had showed them such a stone. So now Dick said, "We'd like you to become an Explorer some time, but don't bring us any more agates. I can find them by the dozen at Fox Hollow." The president of the Explorers Club looked at Jeffrey very closely. "You know something? I don't think you know what our club stands for."

"Yes, I do." Jeff's voice sounded small but determined. "You can't become a member of the Explorers Club until you've discovered something *very* unusual. You found a meteorite, so that makes you the best Explorer. And that's why you're president of the club."

Dick puffed out his chest a little. He was proud

of being president of the Explorers Club. It had come about when he had gone on an expedition by himself and discovered a meteorite near Charlestown, the town where he lived. His picture was shown in the newspaper with the meteorite, which he had given to the Charlestown University for display in their museum. Shortly after that, Dick got the idea of starting the Explorers Club. Up to date there were four members who belonged to the club, and each one felt that he had made a fine contribution as an Explorer.

Now Jack decided it might help if he were to tell Jeffrey of *his* discovery. He had told him about it before, but it would not do any harm to tell him again.

"Gee, Jeff, I wouldn't waste any more time looking for agates. You take the smoked crystal that I found. My uncle believes there isn't another stone like it in Oregon. He is going to exhibit it at the next Mineral Show."

Porky wanted to be heard, too. He was a fat boy with a heart as big as he was round. "I wish I could find another fossil like mine for you, Jeff, but Dad says they're pretty scarce. He has never seen one like the one I found."

"Why don't you look for some petrified wood?" added Toni. "I found my piece at Cedar Grove. Of course, Mother says it is a rare specimen, and she knows because she's a Girl Scout leader."

Jeff listened and with a heavy sigh put the agate back into his pocket. He wondered if he would ever qualify as an Explorer and be able to join the club.

"Come on, Explorers. We'd better get a move on us," said Dick, wanting to show his authority as president of the club. "We've got to make plans for our next expedition."

Jeff watched the Explorers walk away. He waited until they turned into a wide street of houses. Then he began following slowly because he did not want them to think he was trailing them. All he wanted to do was to look at their hut.

Presently, Jeff found himself sitting on a wooden fence that enclosed Dick's back yard. In the middle of the yard stood the famous Explorers hut. It was made from old crates that the Explorers had gathered at supermarkets, and from bits of lumber left from the addition built on to Dick's house. A small American flag waved from a stick nailed to the roof of the hut, and its only door, that wobbled on its hinges every time it was opened, was tightly shut.

Jeff kept looking at the closed door. Slowly he climbed down from the fence and started tiptoeing over to the hut to peek through a wide crack in

the wall. But he had gone only several yards when something bounced on the roof and made a sound like a gun going off.

Jeff turned around and began to run. It was too late. The Explorers poured out of the hut like angry hornets, and before Jeff could climb over the fence, they were at his heels.

"Hey! What's the big idea?" shouted Dick. "We don't like being disturbed when we're having a conference."

Jeff's lips started to quiver. "I didn't do anything. I—"

Before Jeff could finish, the noise came again.

"Look!" cried Toni. "It's a squirrel. He just dropped an apple on the roof. I saw him do it."

"What do you know!" Jack's mouth opened wide with amusement as he watched the squirrel, who was perched in an oak tree that shaded the hut. The animal had pulled down another green apple from a nearby tree and was about to bombard the roof of the hut once more.

"I wonder what those apples taste like?" said Porky, rubbing his stomach as he always did when he was hungry. He walked over to the side of the hut and picked up a green apple from the ground. Dick and Jack joined him, while Toni stayed with Jeffrey.

"I'm glad I found out it was a squirrel," she whispered.

Jeff half smiled.

"Never mind," she told him. "You'll be an Explorer yet. I know you will." She gave Jeff's hand a hard squeeze.

Dick saw Toni trying to comfort Jeffrey. "I'm sorry I blew my top, Jeff," he called.

"That's all right," answered Jeffrey. Then, feeling very shy and deciding he had better go, he climbed over the fence.

He could not help looking back, however, as he walked away. The Explorers were going into the hut, and Jeffrey longed more than ever to be with them.

When he reached the front of Dick's house, he pulled the agate out of his pocket and threw it into a field across the street. After that he started out for Fox Hollow, a small valley surrounded by evergreen trees. Perhaps he would find a fossil there, or a piece of smoked crystal.

Jeffrey liked to go to Fox Hollow even if he didn't find anything. In the spring, birds building their nests were interesting to watch. In the fall, spiders taking off on their silk lines made him wish that he could glide into space.

On this day, however, when Jeffrey reached Fox

Hollow, his attention was attracted to a bed of ferns not far from a path leading into the woods. The ferns were swaying back and forth like tall blades of grass in a windstorm.

Jeffrey decided it must be an animal that was causing the ferns to move. As he drew closer, he could not see any woodland creature. Still the ferns continued to sway.

Then, suddenly, Jeffrey caught a glimpse of a small rabbit. The next thing he knew, the rabbit disappeared.

Convinced that the animal had jumped into a hole in the ground, Jeffrey waded through the bed of ferns to find it. He even got down on his knees and pushed the ferns aside, but he could not see a hole anywhere. Only an uprooted tree lay in front of him.

Before he could investigate the base of the tree, a strange noise filled the air. It sounded muffled and then it grew louder, like the distant roar of waves pounding on a beach.

Jeffrey's heart began to thump. As he put his hands over his ears to soften the noise, he turned cold with fright. The strange figure of a man was coming toward him.

CHAPTER TWO

A Man from Another Planet

Jeffrey could not move—he was so frightened, for the man who had come out of the woods was not an ordinary man. He was a spaceman from another planet. Yes, he looked exactly like the pictures of spacemen Jeffrey had seen in the books he had at home. Only this man was real. He was alive.

Rocking from side to side, the spaceman came slowly toward Jeffrey. He was wearing a diver's suit, heavy boots, and a helmet over his head with an amber glass window in the front of it. Jeffrey could even see the man's space gloves with no fingers on them, only tools that looked like claws.

Suddenly the spaceman turned and walked back to the path. Jeffrey kept his eyes fastened on him until he disappeared among the trees. Then the boy started to run home pell-mell.

Brush scratched his arms and face. He did not stop, though, until he reached a meadow where he fell to the ground, exhausted. He lay there, resting and thinking of the stories he had read about people seeing flying saucers. Yet no one, as far as he knew, had seen a spaceman on this earth, and in Charlestown, too!

Jeffrey jumped up with joy. "Why, I am an Explorer now! I've discovered a man from another planet."

With a loud whoopee, he started back to the hut to get the Explorers to come and see the spaceman. He hurried, too, for every minute counted and he wanted to reach the Explorers before they left on their expedition.

When he reached the hut and found the door closed, he did not take time to knock on it. Instead, he pulled it open and barged in like a bull on the run. Then he sighed with relief, for the Explorers were still there, huddled together in a circle on the dirt floor.

"Wait until you hear what happened to me!" cried Jeffrey. "I went to Fox Hollow, and there I saw—" He paused to get his breath.

The Explorers stared at Jeffrey, wondering what he was going to say next, for they had never seen him act like this before. He was always so shy.

"I saw a spaceman from another planet," continued Jeffrey. He spread his legs apart and dug his hands into his pockets with importance.

Dick laughed loudly. "Ah, come now, Jeff. You don't expect us to believe that! You've been reading books about space travel."

"Yes, I have some books at home, but I saw a spaceman. Honest, I did."

There was silence from the Explorers. Dick picked up a piece of straw and with an amused smile began chewing on it. Jack sighed and shrugged his shoulders. He was getting tired of Jeffrey, his agates, and now the crazy idea that he had seen a man from outer space.

Toni felt differently about Jeffrey. Her mother had told her that he was lonely because he had no brothers and sisters to play with. So now, rather than embarrass Jeffrey by staring at him, she busied herself writing numbers in the soft dirt with a stick.

Porky joined her, for he also did not want to make Jeffrey feel uncomfortable, although he doubted very much that he had seen a spaceman.

Jeffrey, however, was not going to be sidetracked now—not when he had qualified to become an Explorer.

"Please come to Fox Hollow," he said. "I'll prove to you that there is a spaceman there. I saw him with my own eyes."

Still silence from the Explorers.

Then Jeffrey had an idea. "Since you don't believe me, I'm going to the newspaper office and talk to the photographer there. He'll listen to me."

This was all Dick needed to hear. He remembered only too well how eager the photographer had been to take his picture when he had found the meterorite. And now, if Jeff were telling the truth about the spaceman, it would be fun to have all the Explorers in on the discovery.

Dick looked Jeffrey square in the eyes and asked, "Are you dead sure you saw a spaceman? You're not fooling us, are you?"

"Oh, no! I wouldn't fool you," cried Jeff. "I really saw a spaceman from another planèt."

"All right then," said Dick. "Come on, Explorers. This should be an interesting expedition. I'll lead the way to Fox Hollow and from there you will take over, Jeff."

Jeffrey nodded, hardly believing his ears. Dick was already talking to him as if he were an Explorer. And he was one. He had made his contribution. He had discovered a spaceman from another planet.

With buoyant steps, Jeffrey hurried with the Explorers to Fox Hollow.

"Where do we go from here, Jeff?" asked Dick when they had reached the hollow.

Jeffrey looked over at the bed of ferns and then at the path leading into the dark woods.

"The spaceman came out of there," he whispered, pointing to the path.

"So that's his hideout!" Dick turned to Jeffrey, waiting for him to lead the way.

Jeffrey stared at the path with the tall trees on both sides of it. He took several steps, and then looked back at Dick.

"Okay, I'll take over." Dick motioned for the Explorers to follow.

In single file, with Jeffrey behind Dick, the small group walked silently along the trail. As they went deeper into the woods, they kept looking on both sides, expecting to see the spaceman any moment. Instead, a loud, roaring noise broke the stillness.

Dick was the first to speak. "Gosh! What's that?"

he shouted to make himself heard.

"I forgot to tell you," Jeff shouted back. "I heard that noise just before I saw the spaceman."

"He must be around here then," decided Dick.

Jeff nodded. The others said nothing, but their silence told Jeffrey they were impressed, and he felt better. Even Dick had a strange look and beads of perspiration stood out on his forehead.

Jeffrey then heard Dick's commanding voice. "Come on, Explorers. It's now or never." And Dick advanced farther along the path.

Jeffrey followed with the others. He could see a clearing at the end of the trail now. That was not all, either. Something big loomed up ahead—something that neither he nor the Explorers could make out. But stealthily, like cats pursuing their prey, the group continued until Dick motioned for them to stop behind some low brush.

For a moment the Explorers were too bewildered to realize what they were seeing in the clearing below. Then, gradually, their eyes focused on several spacemen standing near a space ship. It was resting on a supporting table, and it looked like an enormous whale with a huge window in the middle and many tiny windows in the front.

Not far from the space ship was a streamlined rocket, and next to it was a space platform which

resembled the wheel of a gigantic truck. On the rim of the wheel spacemen were working at an instrument board.

"Jeepers!" shouted Jack above the loud noise. "I'll bet they came from Mars."

"I'll bet they did!" Dick rubbed his hands with excitement. "Boy! Is this a scoop for us! We're the first ones in this world to see men from outer space!" He turned to Jeff and grinned. "You certainly weren't fooling. You are one of us. You're an Explorer now."

Jeff grinned back, and with a joyful face he watched the scene below. The loud noise had stopped, but the big wheel of the space station had begun to move.

"Look at all the spacemen on that wheel!" cried Toni. She leaned over and stared wide-eyed as the wheel turned on its axis, showing spacemen in separate rooms. Some were seated at desks, talking into telephones. Others were stretched out on comfortable chairs, reading books and magazines. And some were sitting at tables, eating.

"I wish they would give us some of their food," muttered Porky, suddenly realizing he was hungry.

No one said anything, for just then the wheel stopped moving and some spacemen sprang into action. They started climbing the stairs to the hub of the gigantic wheel.

Jeff watched spellbound. This was something more wonderful than he had expected to find. Why, it was like seeing a strange city from another world revolving on a big wheel!

Then he heard Jack say, "Hey, Dick. If the spacemen should suddenly decide to return to their planet, no one will believe we saw them. So we had better go and get witnesses right away."

"Yes, we'd better," added Porky. "They'll probably leave the big wheel, but I wonder how they got it here in the first place."

Jack frowned. "You've got something there. How did they get the big wheel here?"

Dick had been looking around, engrossed in everything that he saw. "Look!" he cried. "There are cameras down there near the trees. We're not seeing men from Mars! A Hollywood studio is making a movie here. That's what they're doing. They are on location."

"Oh, dear! I was sure they were spacemen from Mars." Toni's voice sounded so disappointed.

Jack was more put out than disappointed. "Gosh! Now our expedition is a flop."

Dick nodded and gave an unhappy sigh.

Jeffrey groaned loudly.

"Never mind, Jeff," said Toni. "It's exciting to

see, anyway. I've never watched a movie company on location."

"Neither have I," said Porky. "So cheer up, Jeff."

Jeffrey was sad, though, for all he could think of was that his wish to become an Explorer had not come true. And yet, he told himself, Dick might still let him belong to the club. He just might.

Meanwhile, they all wanted to see more of the movie company and circled around it, staring and watching until one of the men motioned them off.

On the way home, Jeffrey decided to talk to Dick about the club.

"Am I still an Explorer?" he asked.

Dick hesitated. "I don't know what to answer, Jeff. You see, you really didn't discover a spaceman."

Jeffrey said no more until they reached the end of the path. Then, remembering the rabbit in the bed of ferns, he turned to his friend. "Dick, I know a place where we could have an exciting expedition."

"We don't want to hear about another one of your expeditions," interrupted Jack.

"I do," said Dick.

But Jack had no intention of listening to Jeffrey, and to get Porky and Toni's attention, he started teasing them with a stick and making them run.

Jeffrey was glad to be left alone with Dick. "You see that bed of ferns over there," he said, pointing to it.

Dick nodded and Jeff went on. "Before I saw the spaceman, there was a rabbit moving around in those ferns. And then the strangest thing happened. The rabbit suddenly disappeared. I know rabbits often jump into holes in the ground, but this rabbit just dropped out of sight because I couldn't find a hole in the ferns anywhere."

Dick immediately showed interest. "We'll have to investigate where the rabbit went, Jeff. It might be—"

Dick did not finish, for just then a loud cry pierced the stillness. It was Toni screaming that she had seen a snake.

"It's the biggest snake I ever saw," she said to Dick and Jeffrey when they came up to her at the other end of Fox Hollow. Porky and Jack were trying to locate the reptile, and Dick and Jeffrey joined them. They all poked around with sticks in the brush for quite awhile.

"Ah, there is no snake here," said Jack, finally. He was no longer excited.

"There is, too!" cried Toni. "I saw it. It was this long." She stretched her arms way out to give the length.

Jack laughed and began imitating Toni when she had first seen the snake. He squealed and ran around in a circle holding his chest.

Toni did not think Jack was amusing. With flying arms and legs she was about to jump on him.

Dick came to the rescue and separated the two Explorers, but they were still not very friendly when everyone left a few moments later. They tagged behind, passing jeering remarks to each other.

Jeffrey took this chance to speak to Dick again. "Shall I come to the hut tomorrow, Dick? Then maybe we could make plans for another expedition. The one I told you about, where the rabbit disappeared in the bed of ferns, could be very exciting. We might discover something out of this world."

"Yes, Jeff, that's possible. Only you're not an Explorer yet. The spaceman you saw was make-believe."

Jeffrey was silent. His eyes showed his disappointment.

"Don't feel bad, Jeff," put in Porky, giving him a friendly cuff under the chin.

Then Dick said, "I'll tell you what we'll do, Jeff. We'll hold a meeting and cast a vote to see how the Explorers feel. We might be able to make an exception and let you join our club after all."

"Whoopee! That would be swell!" Jeffrey spun around like a top and kicked up the dirt with his feet.

"We'll vote as soon as we get back to the hut," promised Dick.

When the Explorers reached the hut, however, it was six o'clock. As soon as they learned the time, Toni, Porky, and Jack started for home, running as fast as they could. Jeffrey hurried, too. He was afraid his mother might have called the police department to look for him. She had done that once before when he had been late coming home from school.

On the way home, the only person Jeffrey could see was a man walking ahead of him through the field. His dark blue suit stood out among the high grass, and his bald head glistened in the late sunlight like a mirror.

Soon Jeffrey caught up with the stranger. He padded along in back of him, until suddenly the man stopped.

"Excuse me," said Jeffrey as he bumped into him trying to pass him.

The man turned and glared at Jeffrey. Then he pulled a handkerchief out of his pocket and blew his nose. At this point something else came out of his pocket—a photograph that fell to the ground.

Jeffrey picked it up. It was a picture of the Explorers hut.

"Hey! Give me that!" demanded the stranger. His voice was high pitched and squeaky for a man. He snatched the photograph out of Jeffrey's hand, turned on his heel, and walked rapidly away.

Jeffrey's mouth stood wide open. The stranger certainly was concealing something, he decided, for what was he doing with a picture of the Explorers hut?

Baffled, Jeffrey hurried on, until he passed the man. He stopped, peered at him through his heavy glasses, and then sprinted toward home to make up for lost time.

CHAPTER THREE

Jeff Meets the Stranger Again

It was not until the next afternoon that Jeff was able to go to the hut. In the morning he had a dental appointment, and after that a shopping tour with his mother. He went to store after store and tried on clothes to make sure they fitted. All the while he felt as jumpy as a Mexican jumping bean, for he was anxious to find out if the Explorers had voted in his favor.

So his heart pounded in his chest as he climbed over the fence into Dick's back yard. The door of the hut was closed but he could see a white envelope sticking out from a small crack. As he drew nearer, he found that it had his name on it—Jeff Jones written in big letters.

With excited fingers, Jeff opened the envelope and pulled out a piece of paper. Dick had written him a note. In a mumbling voice Jeffrey read it aloud:

"Dear Jeff. I am sorry that all the Explorers did not vote in favor of your joining our club. It is my duty to tell you this. Dick Wright. President of the Explorers Club."

Jeffrey crumpled up the piece of paper and threw it on the ground. Downcast, he walked to the fence, climbed over it, and sat under a tree. He amused himself with an old twenty-five cent piece that his father had given him that morning.

On his last birthday Dad had presented him with a book about collecting old coins. Ever since then Jeffrey had studied every coin that came into his possession. One coin, which he was proud of, was a 1913 Buffalo nickel with an "S" on it. It was worth five dollars according to the book.

Now Jeffrey wondered what the old quarter was worth, since it was dated 1853. He held the coin up to the light and examined it from every angle. Then, suddenly feeling someone in back of him, he turned around with a start. To his surprise he found himself looking up at the man he had met in the field yesterday. The man was smiling.

"That looks like an old coin you've got there," he said to Jeffrey. His voice sounded as squeaky as the day before. "Let me see the coin," he added, still smiling. I might be able to tell you if it's valuable."

Jeffrey hesitated. The man's sudden friendliness puzzled him. So he got slowly to his feet and eyed the stranger in silence.

Finally, the man winked at Jeffrey and gave a loud laugh that showed three gold teeth in his mouth.

This so startled Jeffrey that his own mouth stood wide open, too. Then he began to laugh. He really did not know why he was laughing. It was just that the stranger made him feel that way.

"Come on, now. Let me see that old coin you've got," urged the man. "I've made a study of old coins, and I know quite a bit about them."

"You do!" Jeff felt he was on more familiar ground now.

"Sure," said the stranger. "Some old coins are

worth a lot of money. Collectors will pay a good price for them." He pulled a magnifying glass out of his pocket. "Let me take a look at that old quarter."

Jeff handed him the coin. "Dad gave it to me this morning. And I've got a 1913 Buffalo nickel. It's worth five dollars because of the 'S' on it. The letter stands for the San Francisco mint." Jeffrey proudly tilted his head. "We have only two mints in the United States now. One is at Philadelphia, the other is at Denver. The mint at San Francisco was discontinued after March 1955."

"Ah! So you not only collect coins, but you know a lot about them," said the stranger.

Jeffrey looked pleased. "Coin collecting is an interesting hobby."

"It's a profitable one, too," added the man. "It always surprised me, though, how few people stop and study the coins that they receive in change when they buy things. Many valuable old coins pass through their hands without their knowing it."

Jeff listened and watched the man study his quarter under the magnifying glass.

"Do you think it's worth a lot of money?" he asked him. "I was going to see how it is listed in my coin book when I got home, but perhaps you can tell me now what it is worth."

The man turned the old quarter over in the palm of his hand. "This is the Liberty Seated type of quarter," he said. "I'm not certain, though, that it's a collector's item." He examined the coin some more.

Jeff decided that the stranger was taking a long time to find out if the coin was valuable, especially since he claimed to know so much about the subject.

"Have you collected many old coins?" he asked him.

"Yes," replied the man. "Unfortunately I had to sell them because I needed money. At present I don't have a collection, but I wish I did."

Jeff was about to ask another question when suddenly two cats started to fight nearby. One was a tomcat. The other was a white cat called Chinny that belonged to Dick's mother. It was her pet, and when she was not at home, Molly, the cook, took charge of Chinny.

Jeff's eyes opened wide as he watched the two cats snarl and spit and cuff each other with fur flying in all directions. He wanted to help Chinny, who was getting the worst of the battle, but he did not know what to do.

The stranger came to the rescue. He picked up a stick and struck the tomcat—not very hard, but enough to make the animal dart away like a streak of lightning.

"You can't hurt tomcats," he said to Jeff. "They are as tough as shoe leather."

Jeffrey nodded, and grabbed Chinny, who was still within reach. Then he climbed over the fence and gave the cat to Molly, who had come running outside when she heard the commotion. With Chinny in her arms, the cook examined the cat from head to tail. Except for a few missing chunks of hair, Chinny seemed to be unharmed.

With a relieved sigh, Molly thanked Jeffrey and asked him into the kitchen for some cookies.

"Gee, thanks," said Jeff, "but it was that man who rescued Chinny. Boy, you should have seen him whack the tomcat with a stick."

Molly was stroking Chinny and nestling her face in the cat's soft fur. "Then it sure was a good thing that man was there, Chinny. Otherwise, you would be a sad cat."

Jeff agreed and ran out of the house to tell the stranger how much Molly appreciated his coming to the rescue.

"Hey, Mister," he called, looking all around for him. But the man was nowhere in sight, and as Jeff stood there, wondering where he could have gone, a thought flashed through his mind. In the excitement the stranger had gone off with his old quarter, and he did not know his name or where he lived. Then another thought came to Jeff. His coin might be very valuable!

Jeffrey could hardly wait to look at his coin book to find out. So he hurried home and dashed up to his room.

His mother, surprised at his sudden appearance, followed him to see what it was all about. But Jeffrey already had his nose buried in his coin book.

"I knew it!" he cried aloud. "That old Liberty Seated quarter is worth fifty dollars. Do you hear that, Mom? It's worth fifty dollars. And now that man has gone off with it, and I'll probably never see him again." Jeffrey whacked the pillow on his bed in exasperation.

"Why not wait until your father comes home," his mother suggested. "He might have some good ideas."

So the boy decided to wait until dinner to discuss the matter of his coin with Dad.

"It's too bad you don't know the man's name," said his father at the table after Jeffrey had told him what had happened. "Since he is a coin collector, he must have known what your old quarter is worth."

"Then he didn't forget to give it to me," said Jeff. "He kept it on purpose."

"We'll give him the benefit of a doubt," said Mr. Jones. "If he's an honest person, he'll see that you get your coin back, even though he doesn't know your name. You said that he had a picture of the Explorers hut, so perhaps he will give it to Dick, thinking he knows you. Of course, I don't know why he would have a photo of the hut in the first place. Maybe he likes to take pictures. By the way, I had lunch with Dick's father today. He was telling me about this hut and the Explorers Club. You are a member, aren't you?"

"Er—no. Not yet," answered Jeff. "I almost became a member yesterday. I thought I had discovered a spaceman from another planet."

"A spaceman, eh?" Mr. Jones tried to hide a smile.

"Yeah. Only it wasn't a real spaceman. You see, they are making a movie near Fox Hollow about spacemen, rockets, and stuff."

"I heard about that," said his father. "And you thought a space ship had landed from Mars?"

"Well, yes." Jeff toyed with his food. He did not feel very hungry now that he had lost his coin and his chance to join the Explorers Club.

His mother looked at him in concern. "Aren't you going to eat your dinner, dear?"

Before Jeff could make an excuse, his father said,

"What do you have to do to belong to the Explorers Club?"

Jeff quickly explained how hard it was to get in the club and what you had to do to join.

"If I were you, I'd hunt for a hummingbird's nest," suggested his father. "I am sure no one around here has seen any because they are not easy to find."

Jeff was all ears. "Where do I look for a hummingbird's nest?"

Mr. Jones had a faraway expression. "When I was a boy I used to collect all kinds of nests. I remember climbing to the top of a maple tree to get a white-faced hornet's nest. It had been hanging there all winter, so I knew there were no hornets in it. I'll never forget the look on the teacher's face when I took it to school. She thought it was filled with hornets." Mr. Jones laughed and Jeffrey laughed, too. He loved to hear his father tell stories about his boyhood.

Jeffrey wanted to hear more about the hummingbird's nest. "What does a hummingbird's nest look like, Dad?"

"It's about the size of a chestnut," answered his father. "It's made of soft plant down and is covered with lichens. You can hardly see it against the bark of a tree. Sometimes you'll find the nest in a tall tree."

"Gee! I'm glad you told me, Dad. I'll climb ten trees until I find one."

His mother looked frightened. "Oh, no, Jeffrey. Please don't."

"What's wrong, Alice?" said Mr. Jones. "Jeff certainly is old enough to climb a tree."

"Sure I am," answered Jeff.

After dinner Mr. Jones went into the living room to watch a play on TV with Mrs. Jones, and Jeffrey was left alone, thinking that tomorrow he would climb the tallest tree he could find and look for a hummingbird's nest.

CHAPTER FOUR

Mystery at Dick's House

The next day Jeffrey slipped quietly out of the house while his mother was talking on the telephone. He knew that her phone conversations were always lengthy. So he took the opportunity to get away without being asked where he was going. After last night's talk on tree climbing, he knew his mother's fears on the subject. Still Dad had said he could climb trees, and it was important that he look for a hummingbird's nest. For this reason Jeffrey hurried along, eager to find the tallest and biggest tree in Charlestown.

He soon found a fir tree not far from Dick's house. It was perfect, he decided, for the Explorers might see him, and he was sure they had never climbed a tree as big as this one.

With a shrill whistle Jeff started to hoist himself up the trunk of the tree. Finding it not so difficult as he had expected, he climbed higher, and at the same time he kept looking for the tiny nest of a hummingbird.

A woman, out with her dog, stopped and watched Jeffrey. Soon her interest attracted others, and before long Jeffrey had an audience. He could hear them talking about him, but he did not look down. He just kept climbing higher and higher.

Finally, a man's voice, sounding louder than the others, called to Jeffrey, "Young fellow, how far are you going?"

"I'm going to climb to the top of the tree," answered Jeff.

"Oh, you mustn't!" cried an old lady. "It's too dangerous. You might fall."

Jeff chuckled. This was all he needed to hear, for now that he had found tree climbing an easy task, he wanted to test himself. Besides, it was thrilling to have people watch him. Never in all his life could he remember receiving so much attention, and he was enjoying every minute of it. He even forgot to look for a humming bird's nest—his one object being to make the spectators think he was very brave.

With a little bit more effort, Jeff finally reached the very top of the chestnut tree. Slowly, ever so slowly, he turned around and looked below. A sickening feeling came over him and he blinked, startled. The group of people appeared small and blurred, and he clung to the branch of the tree for all he was worth.

"Come on down, sonny," called the man. "You've done enough tree climbing for one day."

"I should say he has," retorted the old lady. "Why, he scares the daylight out of me up there so high."

Jeffrey swallowed hard. He suddenly discovered that he was afraid to come down.

"What's the matter with him?" asked the old lady.

"I don't know," answered a woman. "He's Jeffrey Jones. I think I had better go and get his mother."

Jeff winced. "Don't do that!" he cried. "I'm coming down."

He took a deep breath but could not budge an

inch. One false step, he told himself, and he would go flying down to the pavement. What should he do?

The people were stretching their necks, anxiously waiting.

"I'll get his mother to call the fire department," said the woman. "They'll get him down."

Beads of perspiration stood out on Jeffrey's forehead. Perhaps he could make it before the hook-and-ladder truck arrived, for it would be very humiliating to face all those people. He tried to get to the branch below. It was no use. He was trembling now from head to toe.

Then, suddenly, he heard Porky's voice. "Stay where you are, Jeff. I'm coming up."

Porky, much against the protests of the crowd, began climbing up the tree. When he reached the top, he held out his hand to Jeffrey.

Jeff would not accept it. "I'm not that yellow," he said. "I'll come down in a little while."

"Oh, never mind about later," said Porky. "I'll help you to get down."

Jeffrey and Porky were still arguing when sirens announced the arrival of the hook-and-ladder truck. After that everyone sprang into action. Porky carefully made his exit down the tree, while the big ladder was raised and put into position where Jeffrey

still clung to a branch. A fireman climbed up the ladder, reached out, and helped Jeffrey.

When the boy got down, he was so embarrassed he did not know what to do. Now he would never live down the fact that the fire department had to rescue him from the top of a tree. Oh, why couldn't he be like Porky? The fat boy had not been afraid to climb down from the top of that tree. With these thoughts running through his mind, Jeff turned on his heel and walked away.

Soon he heard voices. His heart began to pound since he recognized that it was some of the Explorers talking.

"Jeff is afraid of his own shadow," said Jack. "I'll bet if I were to say 'boo' he'd run."

"No, he wouldn't," defended Toni. "It's not nice to talk like that about Jeff. My mother said—"

"I don't care what your mother said," interrupted Jack. "Jeff is a scaredy cat. He can't even climb down a tree."

Jeffrey could not bear to see the Explorers now, so he hid behind some bushes near Dick's back door.

The Explorers walked right by his hiding place.

"Let's forget about Jeff. I wish Molly would tell us where Dick is," said Toni. "I'm going to ask her again."

Jeffrey could hear knocking on Dick's kitchen

door. He guessed the Explorers must be taking turns, since there were ten knocks in all.

Then came Molly's voice, loud and distinct. "What! Are you here again? I told you before that Dick isn't home."

"Where did he go?" asked Toni in a polite manner.

"I don't know. Maybe to his grandmother's or to his aunt's. Now I've got things to do. So get along with you, and don't bother me again."

With that the three Explorers hurried off toward the hut.

Jeffrey stretched his cramped legs and, after making sure that the coast was clear, started to crawl out of his hiding place. A bee buzzing around made him draw back, and as he waited for the insect to fly away, his attention was drawn to the window above his head. It was open, and he could hear a man and a woman talking in low voices.

Jeffrey knew he shouldn't listen to their conversation. That would be eavesdropping. His mother had taught him that eavesdropping was bad manners. You should not listen to things you weren't supposed to hear.

Yet Jeffrey could not pry himself away, for the woman was saying in a sobbing voice, "My poor Dick! I just know he is kidnaped."

"Now, dear, don't come to conclusions so quickly," said the man. "Dick probably is lost. So let's wait before we notify the police."

Jeffrey gulped. He could hardly believe that Dick might be kidnaped. Stunned, he heard the next bit of conversation, realizing that it was Dick's mother and father talking again.

"You see, dear, I don't want the police to know about Dick until we are very sure that he has been kidnaped," said Mr. Wright. "This way we can wait for a telephone call. If it's the kidnaper, I'll meet him and give him the money he wants. But if the police start looking for the kidnaper, or if the newspaper prints that Dick has been kidnaped, something might happen."

"You mean something might happen to Dick?" asked Mrs. Wright.

"Get hold of yourself, Laura," said Mr. Wright. "After all, we don't know anything definite yet."

"But what about the anonymous letter you received last week?" said Mrs. Wright. "The kidnaper must have written it, because he did not leave a ransom note, and in the letter he said that if you got control of the Wilson Lumber Mill, you would regret it all your life. You own the mill now. So I'm sure Dick has been kidnaped."

"Now, Laura, you might be wrong. We have no

absolute proof. Dick could be lost."

Mrs. Wright did not answer. She began to cry again, and between her sobs Jeffrey could hear her say, "Dick's bed hasn't been slept in. He's been gone fifteen hours."

Jeffrey gasped. Fifteen hours! That was a long time to be away from home. Then Jeffrey became tense. The telephone was ringing. Was it the kidnaper calling? Jeffrey knew that, rude as it was to listen, he could not leave his hiding place until he found out.

CHAPTER FIVE

The Conference

Five, ten minutes went by as Jeffrey waited to hear if the kidnaper had telephoned. But only silence came from the open window—a silence that made Jeffrey's curiosity prick like a sharp thorn. Finally he heard Molly offering words of sympathy to Mrs. Wright.

"The kidnaper is taking his time, Mrs. Wright. He'll call when he's ready. Meanwhile, I know that

Dick is all right. The good Lord is taking care of him."

Molly's voice had a soothing effect on Mrs. Wright, and she stopped crying.

Jeffrey crawled out of his hiding place, ducked below the window, and dashed to the front of the house. Now that he was in on the secret of Dick's disappearance, he wanted to mull it over in his mind. He walked quickly down the street and passed a man hobbling along with a cane, but Jeffrey did not see him. The boy was so engrossed in his thoughts that he didn't notice anything around him, even a sprinkling truck that chugged slowly along, spraying water close to the pavements.

Presently Jeffrey turned into another street. It was the street where Toni lived, and she was outside jumping rope. She jumped faster when she saw Jeffrey coming. But Jeffrey did not notice her. He walked right by with the same dazed expression.

Toni stopped jumping, and, catching her foot in the rope, she landed on the lawn. In a second she was up. "Hi, Jeff," she called, running after him. "Where are you going?"

No answer from Jeffrey. He kept on walking, looking straight ahead like someone in a trance.

This was too much for Toni. "Where are you going?" she yelled in his ear.

Jeff came to with a start. "Uh? What did you say?"

"I asked you where are you going?" repeated Toni in an irritated voice.

"Er—I don't know. Sorry." And Jeffrey hurried on.

Toni walked along beside him. She matched her footsteps with his, but soon she was out of breath, for Jeffrey was taking big strides. She wondered how long he intended to keep up the pace. Then, too, his silence was getting her on edge. Always she had been able to make Jeffrey talk and he would forget about being shy. Now her friend had a different look about him. His forehead was puckered with wrinkles, and his lips were pressed into a fine line. Toni decided something was troubling him.

"Is it because you couldn't join our club that you won't talk?" she asked, peering at him with an intent expression. "If it is, I'll speak to Dick. I voted for you. Jack didn't, but Dick is president of the club, and he has full say. So he'll fix it for you. I know he will."

Jeffrey looked at Toni without speaking. He had forgotten about his disappointment with the Explorers Club.

"Don't you want to be Explorer?" asked Toni.

"Oh, sure." Jeff's voice was not very enthusiastic.

"Gee, Jeff. You don't sound it! I don't understand you. You go around looking for agates so that you can join our club, and I'll bet you climbed that tree for the same reason."

Jeffrey's eyes flashed. He walked even faster, and Toni, realizing she had said the wrong thing, felt sorry. Still, her inquisitive nature made her keep trotting along beside Jeffrey.

Finally, in a deep, mysterious voice she said, "You know what? I think something is going on at Dick's house. I didn't tell Porky or Jack because they would say I imagined it. But when I asked Molly where Dick was early this morning, she told me she didn't know. Then when I asked her the second time, she said she had told me he wasn't home. Now she didn't tell me that. So I think something is wrong with Dick because he always lets us know if he is going to his aunt's or his grandmother's house."

Jeff burst out with, "Dick's mother thinks he has been kidnaped." The boy groaned after he said it. He had not wanted to tell Toni, but the secret was out and there was nothing he could do about it.

"Kidnaped!" cried Toni.

"Sh! Don't broadcast it!" Jeffrey sounded so annoyed that Toni was afraid to speak for a minute. Then she whispered, "Tell me all about it."

"I don't think I should because it's a matter of

life and death," said Jeffrey. "I will, though, if you promise not to tell anyone."

"I promise." Toni looked so awed that Jeffrey suggested they go behind the school to talk. There no one would hear them since it was vacation time and the playground was deserted.

In a low, intense voice he told Toni what he had heard in the bushes below the window of Dick's house. Of course, he did not mention why he was hiding there, and Toni did not ask. She was too interested hearing about Dick's disappearance.

Then Jeffrey told about the strange man who had taken a picture of the Explorers hut.

"I wonder if he knows what's happened to Dick," said Jeffrey. "He took my old quarter that is worth fifty dollars, and he said he needed money. So he might be working with the kidnaper. If only I knew his name or where he lives! But I don't know a thing about him except that he collects old coins."

"What does he look like?" asked Toni.

"He's bald. He's got three gold teeth, and he talks in a squeaky voice. He had on a blue suit both times that I saw him. I could tell the police this, but Mr. Wright doesn't want them to know about Dick. He's afraid that if Dick has been kidnaped, the police will start looking for the kidnaper. Then something might happen to Dick."

"Oooh!" Toni shuddered. "I wish there was something we could do."

"That's the way I feel. I want to help Dick, but I don't know how." Jeffrey gave a deep sigh.

After that, both children were silent, but they were giving the matter serious thought. Jeffrey kept studying it from every angle. Finally, he stood up and said, "I know Dick's parents won't like it when I tell them I was listening under their window, but I've got to speak to them about that man. I've just got to."

Toni nodded and looked at Jeffrey wide-eyed. He was acting so differently, so grown up, and she admired him as much as she admired Dick.

"I'll go with you," she said.

"No. I must see this thing through alone. Remember, Mr. Wright doesn't want anyone to know about Dick. If he finds out that I've told you, it will make matters worse."

"Ah, gee," said Toni, pouting. "I promised not to tell anyone, and when I make a promise I keep it. So please let me go with you."

Jeffrey was firm, but Toni would not take no for an answer. She followed him to Dick's house, and then she sat on the curbstone while Jeffrey went to the rear and knocked on the kitchen door.

Molly answered. "Dick is not here," she said be-

fore Jeffrey could open his mouth to speak.

"But—but I didn't come to see Dick," explained Jeffrey. "I—I—want to see his father."

"What about?" snapped Molly.

"Er—" Jeffrey did not know whether to tell her or not. So he said the next best thing that came to his mind. "I—want to see him on important business."

"Now look, Jeff. Mr. Wright is busy. Some other time." And she closed the door.

"You don't understand, Molly," cried Jeffrey. "I've got to see him!"

He rushed to the front door, but as he knocked on it, Molly was waiting for him.

"If I catch you here once more, you're going to be a might sorry boy," she scolded, shaking her fist at him. Then she slammed the door in his face.

Toni was up from the curbstone in a flash. "What happened, Jeff? Couldn't you see Mr. Wright?"

Jeffrey shook his head. "Molly certainly can be disagreeable. Yet you should have seen her yesterday when something almost happened to Chinny. Why, she gave me cookies because she thought I had saved Chinny from being hurt by a tomcat. It was that man who really saved Chinny, though. Golly, if only I knew his name."

"I know how you feel," said Toni, trying to be

sympathetic and at the same time wishing she could solve the problem. Cupping her face in her hands, she sat down on the curbstone again. Then she turned around and looked up at the Wrights' house. "Maybe Dick's father has gone to meet the kidnaper," she whispered.

Jeffrey had squatted next to Toni. "No. I saw Mr. Wright when Molly opened the front door, and I saw Mrs. Wright, too. She looked so sad."

"Oh, dear. If only there was something we could do, but we really don't know if Dick has been kidnaped or not."

"That's right," answered Jeff. "I have only circumstantial evidence." Jeffrey was proud of the large word he had rolled off his tongue. Toni looked very impressed. He was about to use another large word when Porky and Jack came bicycling up the street.

"Hey, Toni, have you found out where Dick is?" asked Jack, bringing his bicycle up to the curb.

Porky skidded to a stop on his. "Yeah, where is Dick? I've got to tell him something important about another expedition."

"Why don't you tell me?" asked Jack.

"You're not the president of the Explorers Club," answered Porky. "And all of us have to have a meeting on it. Where is Dick, anyway?"

Toni shrugged her shoulders. "You ought to be able to find out from Molly but she won't tell you."

"I'll bet she'll tell me," boasted Jack.

Leaving his bicycle on the sidewalk, he walked to the back of the house with Porky close at his heels.

A few minutes later the two boys returned. Toni eyed Jack with a smothered chuckle, for she could tell from his scowling expression that he had learned nothing from Molly. She was afraid to question him, though, for fear she might say something wrong. She *must* keep Dick's disappearance a secret. She must, she must, she kept telling herself.

Jack hopped on his bicycle, but he made no move to leave. Holding onto the handlebars, he began speaking his thoughts aloud. "Gosh! Something mysterious is going on, if you ask me."

"It sure is," chimed in Porky. "I think something is wrong with Dick, and Molly doesn't want to tell us."

Toni gulped, looked knowingly at Jeff, and then quickly turned away.

Jeff did not blink an eyelash. He sat there, still as a statue, until Toni's next remark made him jerk back in alarm.

"Something could have happened to Dick," she chirped in a light voice. Then, catching herself, she added, "No! No! He's probably gone to his grandmother's house. Molly is just cross today because she has a lot of work to do." Toni got up and started tap dancing on the sidewalk. She even turned several handsprings—anything to get away from the puzzled looks of Porky and Jack.

"What's the matter with you, Toni?" asked Porky. "You're acting very strange."

Jack was more direct in his questioning. "You know something about Dick, don't you?" He got off his bicycle and grabbed Toni by the shoulders.

"You leave me alone, Jack Pierce. You're an old bully. That's what you are!" Toni fled down the street, leaving the three boys staring after her.

Porky was bewildered, for he never knew what Toni was going to do next, while Jack was angry that she did not tell him what she knew about Dick. He was certain she knew something. Perhaps Jeff was in on the little game, he decided. After all, they were talking together a while ago.

"What do you know about Dick, Jeff?" said Jack in a stern voice. "Come on. Come clean."

Jeff raised an eyebrow. "You take a lot for granted, don't you?"

"What?" snorted Jack. He had expected Jeff to cringe under his questioning.

"Just what I said," snapped Jeff. "You take a lot for granted." And getting up from the curb, he dug his hands into his pockets and walked calmly down the street. Inwardly, though, he was trembling.

Back on the curbstone Porky grinned from ear to ear. With a twinkle in his eyes he said to Jack, "I guess you can't bully Jeff any more."

Jack did not answer. He was fuming, ready to explode, but rather than let the explosion come, he hopped on his bicycle and zoomed down the street like a streak of lightning. He passed Jeffrey, but the boy did not so much as look his way. He had more important things on his mind. One was Toni. He must speak to her and make her realize, more than ever, that she must keep Dick's disappearance a secret.

CHAPTER SIX

Jeff Gets an Idea

That night Jeff tossed in his bed and finally got up for a drink of water. He had not slept since he turned in an hour ago. This was unusual, for Jeff usually slept well, but he never had things troubling him as he did now. After the curbstone meeting, Toni and he had kept watch at the Wrights' house, waiting to see if Dick's father was going to meet the kidnaper. At nightfall their vigil had come to an end, but from the quietness of the house, they knew that Dick had not returned. Their concern for him was great.

Right now as Jeff thought about Dick a lump swelled in his throat, for he could not put his friend out of his mind. He had tried to talk to Dick's father again, but Molly refused to let him see Mr. Wright. And as for going to the police—Jeffrey dared not do that. Yet he could not help wondering if Mr. Wright was wise in keeping Dick's disappearance a secret.

Jeffrey dared not think any more about his friend. He got back into bed and closed his eyes. He finally slept little that night but at seven o'clock in the morning he was in the kitchen, opening and closing the refrigerator with such noise that he awakened his mother.

"Goodness! What's wrong, Jeffrey?" she cried, hurrying into the kitchen, her hair up in curlers, her robe clutched around her.

"I'm as hungry as a bear," said Jeff.

"It's only seven o'clock. You never get up at this hour. Now go back to bed."

"But Mom, I'm hungry. I can make my own breakfast." Jeff slapped a piece of bread into the toaster.

Mrs. Jones shook her head. "I declare, Jeffrey,

you're acting very strangely these days. Last night we could not get a word out of you at dinner, and now you're up very early. Do you feel all right?"

"Sure. I'm fine." Jeff broke an egg into the frying pan.

His mother watched him a moment and then with another shake of her head left the kitchen. Jeff finished getting his breakfast, but all the time he ate it his mind worked at top speed.

Suddenly an idea came to him. He waved his fork in mid-air, and then sat very still. It was just an idea, he told himself. There might be nothing to it. Yet it could happen. Yes, sir, it could happen!

For the next few minutes Jeff was busy opening and closing kitchen cabinet drawers. He kept his eyes on the door, though, just in case his mother should return. Later he would explain to her the reason for loading his pockets, but now he didn't want to talk. Cookies, a banana, two muffins, and three candy bars made his pockets bulge like big round apples. He even took a brown paper bag, and, after stuffing it with a thermos bottle of water and a flashlight with extra batteries, he set out on a journey that he felt was the most important mission of his life.

His first stop was Dick's house. The early morning air felt cool and refreshing as he squatted on the curbstone in front. He was restless, though, and could hardly wait for eight o'clock to come.

Finally, the chimes on the courthouse rang out the hour. Jeff jumped up from the curb. With head high, he walked up the path to Dick's house and knocked on the front door.

It was not long before Molly's face peered at him through a window on the porch. Jeff looked back at her, solemn as an owl, but Molly's worried expression gave him his answer. Dick had not returned. So Jeff lost no time continuing on his way. He hurried, too, for he wanted to reach Fox Hollow as quickly as possible.

When he walked into the small valley, a flock of crows circled overhead. Their cawing voices were quite a contrast to the roaring noise caused by the movie studio on location a few days ago. Jeffrey had forgotten about that. His one thought was to go to the bed of ferns where the rabbit had disappeared. But instead of looking among the ferns for a hole in the ground, Jeffrey immediately began to hunt around the uprooted tree that lay on the ground close by. To his delight he soon found a dark hole, about two feet wide, at the base of the tree. It was almost completely covered by grass and leaves and fallen branches.

"I knew it!" he cried. "The rabbit jumped into this hole."

Jeffrey cleared the rubbish away from the hole and then aimed his lighted flashlight into the dark cavity. All he could see, though, was a slope going farther and farther into the blackness below. Where it went he did not know.

He lay on his stomach and peered again into the yawning cavity. A current of air brushed against his warm face. Then he pricked up his ears and turned around, as a familiar voice called his name.

It was Toni. Jeff got to his feet and watched her wade through the bed of ferns.

"I've been hunting everywhere for you," she said, looking hurt. "Why didn't you tell me you were going to Fox Hollow?" Then curiosity made her bubble with questions. "Are you trying to track down the kidnaper? Do you have some clues?" She did not wait for Jeffrey to reply, for her eyes opened wide as she stared into the hole at the foot of the uprooted tree. "Golly! What a big hole! Is the kidnaper hiding Dick down there?" she added in a whisper.

Jeff did not answer. He was bracing himself for the plunge into the dark earth underneath. Before Toni was able to continue her conversation, he crawled headfirst into the hole.

Inch by inch he moved down the slope, carrying his lighted flashlight in one hand and pulling the paper bag after him with the other.

With a worried look, Toni watched the last of Jeffrey disappear down the dark hole. Then she let out a loud yell. "Wait for me!" Quickly she muffled her mouth, afraid someone might have heard her. Still, she meant what she said, and she soon followed Jeffrey into the blackness below.

Jeffrey heard Toni coming and tried to give her a little light. He was glad of her presence. At the same time, though, he was afraid that the darkness would terrify her since it was not like the usual night when the moon often brightened the leaves on the trees. This darkness was very black. It closed in on all sides and made Jeff feel that an unseen hand was about to reach out grab him.

Yet somehow Jeffrey managed to move forward, for he kept telling himself that he must for Dick's sake. His friend's life was at stake, and every minute was precious.

Finally, Jeff came to the end of the slope. To his surprise he saw that it turned into a tunnel, the blackest tunnel he had ever seen in his whole life.

"I'm scared," whispered Toni. "Let's not go any farther."

"I must," answered Jeffrey. And with determination he had never shown before, he started to wriggle through the narrow tunnel.

Toni hesitated. She was afraid to go back alone, so she moved like an inchworm along the dark passageway after Jeffrey.

Suddenly the tunnel opened into a wider passageway with a stream on one side of the floor. Jeffrey and Toni found they could stand up. The ceiling just touched their heads. It was a glorious feeling to be able to stretch their arms and legs. But the darkness ahead loomed up more dense than ever, and the flashlight in Jeffrey's hand shook as he sent a beam into the unknown.

"Do you think we'll find Dick?" whispered Toni. "Maybe the kidnaper—" She caught her breath, for she saw a white bug near the water.

Now there were two things that Toni did not like —snakes and bugs. Why? She did not know, but she did, and this was such a strange-looking bug! She grabbed Jeff's arm and pointed to the white creature that remained motionless on a rock.

"It's only a cricket," said Jeff.

"A cricket is black," protested Toni.

"Not this one," answered Jeff with authority. "That's a long-legged cricket, and it's blind. I know because I've read about it in a book in the library.

This cricket is one of the cave dwellers, and it's white because it lives underground."

"Golly! Then this tunnel must be part of a cave!" Toni was excited. She had never been in a cave.

Neither had Jeffrey, and, although the passageway ahead looked very black, he started to move on. Toni tagged after him. She was still scared, though, and her teeth clicked like marbles in her mouth. If only Jeffrey would turn back, she kept telling herself.

But Jeffrey continued to walk through the long tunnel that twisted and turned like a scenic railway with a stream running along one side of it. Toni kept looking away from the stream. She was afraid she might see another long-legged cricket.

Presently the long tunnel swerved to one side and opened into an unexpected sort of underground room. Hand in hand Jeffrey and Toni went into the room. They stood there, amazed.

"It's like fairyland!" cried Toni breathlessly, as she watched the beam from Jeff's flashlight show walls of stone flowers. Some were shaped like lilies, others like roses.

On the uneven floor of the room, little pools of water were scattered about like the tide pools at the beach. Coral-like pebbles danced on the bottom of the pools that were edged with lacy films of lime.

Then Jeffrey turned his flashlight on the ceiling of the room.

"Look at the icicles hanging from the ceiling!" cried Toni.

"They're not icicles," corrected Jeff. "They are stalactites."

Toni frowned. She had never heard that word before. "What did you say they were?" she asked.

"Stalactites," repeated Jeff. "Of course they do look like icicles, but they are made of rings of lime. You see, they are caused by drops of water clinging to the ceiling of the cave. The drops evaporate and leave the lime that was in the water. These are the stalactites."

"Goodness!" said Toni, blinking her eyes, impressed. "You certainly know a lot, Jeff."

The boy smiled, thinking that reading books was worth while after all. He was about to give Toni some more facts about the formation of caves when a strange sound came from an opening on the other side of the room.

Toni heard it, too. She stood very still and listened. Then her heart began to pound. The sound was like someone crying.

CHAPTER SEVEN

Jeff Goes Farther into the Cave

Jeffrey walked across the floor of the cave to the opening. He wanted to find out who was crying.

Toni, with eyes as big as saucers, tiptoed in back of Jeff. She held her breath as he focused his flashlight into another dark passageway.

"Do you see anyone?" she whispered.

Jeff shook his head. "No, but I hear someone crying," he whispered back.

"I do, too," answered Toni. Only her lips moved,

75

for she was afraid even to whisper now.

"I've got to find out who it is," said Jeff.

He walked along a narrow path. Toni followed, and stayed so close behind Jeff that if the boy were to stop suddenly, the two of them would tumble to the floor of the cave.

Soon the crying stopped, and only the dripping of water broke the stillness. It sounded very loud in the silence of the passageway.

Toni put her hands over her ears to soften the noise. She was trembling, for at any second she expected somebody to reach out and grab her.

Jeff was also trembling, but he was trying not to show it. He had made up his mind; he would not turn back. Someone was in the cave, and he was going to find out who it was.

Suddenly a light flickered in the distance.

Cautiously Jeff and Toni moved toward it. They were hand in hand now with Toni squeezing Jeff's hand so hard that it hurt both of them. But neither one said anything, for they could see a figure crouching on a rock.

As they drew closer, the figure became clearer. It was Dick!

"Am I ever glad to see you!" he cried. Then he said no more, for tears streamed down his cheeks and he shook all over.

Jeff and Toni could see that his right foot was caught between two rocks and he could not move it.

"It's all right, Dick," said Jeff in a comforting voice. "Don't cry. We'll get you out of here."

"Sure, we will," said Toni, putting her arm around Dick's shoulders. "And we'll get you out of here before the kidnaper comes back," she added in a loud whisper.

Dick raised his tearstained face and looked at Jeffrey and Toni. "Kidnaper? What do you mean?"

"Your mother thinks you were kidnaped," explained Jeff. He told about the conversation he had heard under the window. "Of course, your father said that there was no absolute proof that you had been kidnaped," he added, "and that you might be lost. When no kidnaper telephoned, I began to realize that maybe you had gone on an expedition by yourself, the way you did when you found the meteorite. You see, I remembered how interested you were in the rabbit that disappeared at Fox Hollow."

Dick smiled and waited for Jeff to go on.

"The more I thought about that rabbit, the more I was convinced that he had gone into a hole at the base of that uprooted tree. So I decided that maybe you had fallen in the hole and couldn't get out. I never guessed, though, that you were trapped in a cave."

"But you did figure out so much, Jeff!" cried Toni. "You're smart." She looked at him with a big grin. Then she frowned. "Why didn't you tell me about it? All this time I've been thinking that Dick was kidnaped."

"I wanted to be sure I was right," answered Jeff. "It was just an idea I had. Your father was right about the kidnaping, though, Dick. You shouldn't jump to conclusions unless you're dead sure, especially about something like that."

Dick nodded. "I'm glad you followed through on your idea, though, because I did go on an expedition by myself. I wanted to see where the rabbit had disappeared. I thought he might have gone into the entrance of a hidden cave, and I wanted to be the first to discover it." Dick looked down, embarrassed. "I'll never go into a cave alone again. I would have starved to death if you and Toni hadn't found me."

"That reminds me," said Jeff. "I brought you something to eat." Proudly he pulled the squashed banana out of his pocket. Then came the cookies, muffins, and chocolate bars in the same condition. "And here's some water," he added, taking the thermos bottle out of the paper bag.

Dick grabbed the thermos bottle and pulled out the cork. In silence Jeffrey and Toni watched him bring the water to his parched lips. After he had taken a long drink, he returned the thermos to Jeff. "That's one thing a fellow can't do without—water. Now for the food." He stuffed some cookies into his mouth.

Jeffrey wished he had emptied the refrigerator, for he was sure his mother would not mind—not if she could see how much Dick was enjoying the cookies. Now for the task of getting Dick's foot out from between the rocks. He looked around for something to use as a tool, but there was none.

Then came Dick's voice, muffled from eating more cookies. "I dropped my chisel, Jeff, if that's what you're looking for. It's on the other side of this rock. I couldn't reach it, and my hammer wouldn't do any good."

In a twinkle Jeffrey, with the stone chisel in one hand and the hammer in the other, started chipping at one of the rocks. His strokes were swift. After a while, though, his arms began to ache, and the hammer fell slowly.

"Rest a bit, Jeff," advised Dick.

"Let me help," offered Toni. "You must be very tired."

Jeff shook his head. "I'm not a bit tired," he answered. He was determined to free Dick's foot even if it took him all day to do it. He chipped off some

more of the rock and at the same time was careful not to hurt his friend's foot.

At last Dick gave a cry of joy. He could pull his foot free. On wobbly legs he stood up, but as he did so, there was a loud crash that re-echoed through the dark passageway.

The children looked at each other, horror-stricken. Then Jeffrey and Dick focused their flashlights in the direction of the noise. They could see that the entrance to the room was closed off. A huge boulder had fallen from the ceiling.

"We're trapped!" wailed Dick. "We'll never get out of here!" He sank to the floor. The strain of being in the cave two nights and a day had begun to show on him, and the thought that now he couldn't leave was more than he could bear. Besides, his foot felt numb, as if it had no life in it.

Jeff and Toni were at his side immediately, their faces white with concern.

"Are you all right, Dick?" they kept asking.

Dick nodded and tried to move his foot. Gradually the circulation came back, and he tottered to his feet once more.

"Don't worry about our being trapped," said Jeff. "There must be another way out of this cave. I'll find it." He was amazed at his own words. Yes, there must be another entrance he knew from the science books he had read, but where? he asked himself. And how would he locate it? Only by going into the darkness alone—a thought that terrified him. Yet he knew that Dick depended on him, and Toni, too. He must find that other entrance. Otherwise, they would all starve to death.

"You stay here with Dick," he said to Toni. "I've got my flashlight and some extra batteries. I'll see where this passageway comes out. I won't be long, either. As soon as I find another entrance, I'll come back and get you."

Toni swallowed hard. "Gee, Jeff, you're brave to go alone. You might get lost." There was fear in her voice.

Jeffrey threw back his shoulders. "I'll be all right," he said. He looked at Dick, who was smiling at him with admiration. "Gee, Jeff, I wish I could go with you."

"No. You stay here and rest your foot."

"Take this ball of twine with you then that I brought along," said Dick. "You can unroll it as you go, and if you get lost, you can find your way back. I've also got some arrowheads that you can use for markers."

"Goodness, you are smart to think of those things," said Toni. "And what is this rope for? It looks like the clothesline my mother uses when she hangs up wash."

"That's what it is," answered Dick. "Mom's clothesline. I brought it along to use as a safety line in case I had to drop down a steep slope. To be a spelunker you have to think of these things." Dick proudly handed over the important articles to Jeffrey.

"Spelunker," repeated Toni, puzzled. "What's that, Dick?"

Jeffrey could not resist answering. "A spelunker is another name for a cave crawler," he explained. "There are quite a few spelunkers in this country. They take all kinds of equipment with them when they are going to explore a cave. A stone chisel, hammer, first-aid kit, lamps, flashlights, and candles. You see, a lighted candle is a test for bad air. When the flame goes out, you know you're in trouble."

"Say! You know quite a bit about spelunkers!" cried Dick, looking at his friend in surprise.

"Jeff knows a lot about caves, too," said Toni. "He reads loads of books."

"Oh, I've only read a few," said Jeff. "I wanted to find out how caves were made."

"How are they made?" asked Toni.

"Tell us, Jeff," urged Dick. He was interested in the subject himself but had not taken the time to find out about it.

Jeff took a deep breath before answering. "When it rains very hard, the water soaks into the ground and sometimes reaches beds of limestone. It drips through the cracks in the stone and the cracks become bigger and bigger. Then two cracks come together, and they grow bigger until a hole is formed. As more water goes through the rock, tunnels are made. And after a while one tunnel meets another tunnel. They cross each other and finally an underground room is made."

"With icicles hanging from the ceiling," added Toni. "No. I mean stalactites," she said.

Jeff smiled. "You pronounced the word correctly, Toni."

Toni looked pleased, but not so pleased as Jeff. He was grinning from ear to ear, for Dick was patting him on the back.

"Gee, Jeff, I didn't know you were an authority on caves," said his friend. "I thought I knew something about them. I was going to explore this cave, but getting my foot caught put a damper on everything." He sank down on a flat rock to rest.

Jeffrey could see how tired he was. "I'm going now," he said. Taking a deep breath, he braced himself for pushing on into farther depths under the earth. "I'll see you," he called as he walked away.

Toni and Dick watched him, his figure getting smaller and smaller, until all they could see was darkness.

"My, but Jeff is brave," said Toni.

"Yes, he is," answered Dick. "I guess we never really knew Jeff. He always reminded me of a scaredy cat, but he isn't."

If Jeffrey could have heard what they said, he would have smiled, for right now he was more scared than he had ever been in his whole life. The fear he had had in the top of the tree was nothing compared to what he was going through now. It was as if he were having a bad dream and was walking through a dark tunnel when suddenly the earth swallowed him up. But Jeffrey told himself that he was not dreaming. He was awake, wide awake, and soon this passageway would end.

He continued onward. Silence fell about him— a silence so complete that even the light from his flashlight seemed to make a noise as it hit the ceiling above him. As he went along, he focused his light on the walls of the passageway and in front of him. Then he blinked his eyes and stared very hard. What was that ahead of him? It looked like a big archway, an archway carved out of solid rock.

With pounding heart Jeffrey walked through the archway. He found himself in a room that was much larger than the one he had been in before. His hand shook as he flashed his light along the floor. There lime formations were growing which he knew were called stalagmites. They looked like candles with melted wax dripping down them. Jeffrey wanted to go over and touch them, but something caught his attention that made him draw back in horror.

CHAPTER EIGHT

The Skeleton

It was the skeleton of an animal that Jeffrey saw in a corner of the big room in the cave. Its eyeless skull and its massive frame with the rib bones sticking out made Jeffrey's heart jump with fright. He turned and hurried out of the room, stumbling, as he did so, over a stone tool and vessel that were lying on the floor near the door. He was too scared to examine them. All he wanted to do was to get away from the skeleton as quickly as possible. So he picked himself up and dashed back into the passage-way.

As he ran along, he began to think more clearly, and he knew that he must return to the big room. If he didn't, he would never find another entrance to the cave, and Dick and Toni were depending on him to do this. Besides, why should he be afraid of the skeleton of an animal? After all, it could not hurt him.

With determined steps, Jeffrey retraced his way. He did not get too close to the skeleton, however. In fact, he darted to the other side of the room and then into another tunnel. He hurried along this until the passageway narrowed down to a ledge that hung over a deep pit. Jeffrey peered over the side of the ledge.

"Glory! What a pit! I'll bet it has no bottom to it!" he said aloud to himself.

He drew back on the ledge, trembling. The thought of crawling along the narrow strip terrified him, and he did not feel he could do it. But grad-ually he grew calmer and cautiously started to move forward. There was nothing to hold onto, so he inched his way, staring straight ahead and count-ing up to a hundred to keep his mind off the deep pit below him.

At last, to his great relief, the ledge widened into a passageway. He was able to move freely now. He got to his feet and walked along for several yards, then came to a stop, where the tunnel branched. He did not know whether to take the path to the right or the one to the left.

Finally, he decided to go right. Using the ball of twine and arrowhead markers to blaze his trail, he continued farther into the cave. He had gone only a short distance, though, when he found that the path came to a dead end. Quickly he went back and followed the other path. This led to another underground room.

It was a small chamber. As the beam from his flashlight danced around the room, Jeffrey was startled to see a workbench and a gas lantern, the kind his father used on camping trips.

He walked over to the workbench to look over what else was on it. There was a propane torch, a tin box that was locked, and a newspaper of a recent date. Jeffrey's eyes sparkled with hope. He felt that he was on the right track at last. Someone had found the way in. All he had to do was to find the same way out!

He flashed his light around the small room and investigated every part of it, but the only exit he could discover was a hole in one of the walls. It was just large enough for him to crawl through. Wriggling, squirming, and pushing for all he was worth, he managed to cover a few feet. Then his joy knew no bounds. A slender shaft of daylight peeked through the opening of another tunnel.

Jeffrey rushed forward, not realizing that the ceiling of the passageway was low. He banged his head, and for a second did not know where he was. Then, after rubbing his head to ease the pain, he got down on his hands and knees and crawled along.

In a short time he reached the outside of the cave and broad daylight! Squinting in the sunlight, he spread his arms out and gave an Indian war cry. No one answered it, but Jeff felt better for it just the same.

He wanted to start out for home, but he knew he must go back into the cave to tell Dick and Toni of his discovery and get them out, too. He moved as fast as he possibly could, for nothing frightened him now, neither the narrow ledge over the deep pit, nor the big room with the skeleton of the huge animal. He even stopped to examine the skeleton, and he looked at the stone tool and bowl near the door since they were different from any he had seen before. He must tell Dick about them.

It was a joyful meeting when Jeff got back to his two friends. Dick, however, was more interested in seeing the skeleton than the stone tool and bowl. In fact, he was so excited that he forgot about his foot aching and his weakness.

"Jeepers! You mean you discovered the skeleton of an animal?"

Jeffrey nodded and dug his hands into his pockets. He felt important. "The skeleton is quite big," he told them. "It looks like a monster. Come on. I'll show it to you. It's on the way out." And he led his friends to the big room.

Toni drew back terrified when she saw the skeleton.

"Oooh! I can't look at it," she cried, quickly covering her eyes.

Dick felt differently. "Jeff, that's a wonderful skeleton! Professor Reppy at the Charlestown University will tell us what kind of animal it was. He knows all about prehistoric animals."

"Then it's a dinosaur," squealed Toni, uncovering her eyes and staring at the skeleton in awe.

"No, it doesn't look like the skeleton of a dinosaur," answered Dick. "Most of them were big with long tails. This skeleton might be the bones of an animal that lived during the Ice Age thousands of years ago when men lived in caves. It might be a saber-toothed tiger, although the skull doesn't show the two large teeth. Anyway, whatever kind of prehistoric animal it is, Jeff, you've made a marvelous discovery. You're now a full-fledged Explorer."

Jeffrey had forgotten about wanting to be an Explorer. So much had happened in the past few days that he had given it little thought. Now that his wish had come true, a feeling of happiness went through him.

Toni joined in congratulating Jeffrey. "I'm so glad you're an Explorer! I know how much you wanted to belong to our club. But you know something else, Jeff? You're no longer afraid of anything. Why, you went and found another entrance to the cave all by yourself! Golly, I couldn't have done that." She held her breath to show Jeffrey how frightened she would have been.

Jeffrey enjoyed the praise he was receiving, although he blushed from ear to ear. Then, becoming businesslike, he said, "We better move along to that other entrance, Dick, because your parents are worried about you. Also, you must be hungry as a bear because I didn't bring you much to eat."

"Chew this bubble gum," said Toni, suddenly remembering that she had a piece in her pocket. "Mother says when you chew gum, you don't feel hungry."

"Thanks," said Dick, chewing the gum fast and then blowing a big bubble that made Toni giggle.

Jeffrey laughed, too, and soon the little party of three continued through the cave with Jeffrey leading the way, feeling very proud of himself.

Suddenly he stopped and listened. The ping, ping of dripping water he was used to, but something else broke the stillness of the passageway. It came from the small room directly ahead, and it was two men talking. The voice of one was squeaky and very familiar to Jeffrey.

Jeffrey snapped off his flashlight and turned to Dick and Toni. "That man who took my old quarter—he's here in the cave!"

"Oooh! He's the one you thought had something to do with kidnaping Dick," said Toni.

"Yes, I sure did. It just shows how you shouldn't jump to conclusions."

"I know," said Toni. "But why don't you call him and tell him you want your quarter back?"

"No, don't call him," cautioned Dick. "It's dangerous to shout in a cave. The noise can bring down a piece of the ceiling. That's what happened when you chiseled at the rock, Jeff, to get my foot loose. The vibration weakened a big boulder. But what's this about a man taking your old quarter?"

Jeffrey explained as quickly as he could about the stranger who had taken his old 1853 quarter that was worth fifty dollars.

"That's a lot of money," said Dick. "I'd certainly make him give me back my old quarter if I were you, although I'm not sure this is the place to do it."

Jeffrey did not answer. He moved forward so that he could hear more clearly the conversation between the two men. Dick and Toni followed.

"I hope you know what you're doing," said the man in a gruff voice.

"Of course I know what I'm doing," snapped the other man. His voice sounded so squeaky that Toni started to giggle, but she quickly put her hand over her mouth to smother it. "I'm a master craftsman at this sort of thing," continued the man. "But it takes time to turn out a nearly perfect replica. It's okay with me, though, if you want to back out, Mr. Redfern."

"I wouldn't think of it," came the answer. "We're to split even. Remember?" The man's voice had a threatening tone to it.

"Maybe he held up a bank," Toni whispered to the boys.

"Yeah, I'll bet both of them are robbers," said Dick. "We've got to tell the police."

Jeffrey had other ideas, but he kept silent.

Just then the man with the gruff voice said, "I'll leave you to your work."

"Wait a minute," said the squeaky voice. "I'll go

with you. I left something in the car."

After that there was the sound of departing footsteps and then silence.

"We've got to act quickly," said Dick.

Jeffrey nodded and led the way to the small room
where the gas lantern now burned brightly on the
workbench, and a shaft of daylight came from a hole
in the lower portion of one of the walls. The opening was just large enough for a man to crawl
through.

Jeffrey wondered why he had not noticed the
hole when he was in the room before. Then he remembered that it was where the end of a log and a
rock were embedded in the wall.

So that's how the men had come into the cave!
They had their own secret entrance—a hole that
they kept plugged up from the outside.

Then Dick called out suddenly. "Say, Jeff, take a
look at this!" His friend had gone to the workbench
and was peering at the contents of the tin box,
which was now unlocked. The cover to the box was
lying on the floor.

Jeff quickly joined Dick, and Toni hurried over,
too. With heads bumping into one another, the
children stared at the contents of the box: a magnifying glass, several delicate instruments and den-
tist drills, and a couple of small bottles filled with

liquid. It was all very puzzling to them until Jeffrey noticed a small bronze object on the workbench. It wasn't there before, but he recognized immediately that it was a mold for making coins.

"That guy who took my old quarter must be a counterfeiter!" he cried. "And he uses this cave for a secret hideout. See, here's the mold for making coins, and the rest of the equipment is in the box. Those bottles contain acids and chemicals. I've read in my book at home about counterfeiters making rare coins. They sell them to collectors. Sometimes they get a lot of money for them—thousands of dollars."

"You don't mean it!" exclaimed Dick.

"Yeah, that's right," answered Jeff. "And I'm dead sure that guy is a counterfeiter. He said he was a master craftsman. I wonder what rare coin he's going to imitate? Maybe it will be mine!"

Jeffrey was interrupted by a noise, and the next thing he knew, a pair of legs began to come down through the hole in the wall.

Quick as a flash the children dashed back into the dark passageway, for there was no time to wriggle through the small opening on the other side. They made their getaway just as the stranger dropped to the floor of the small room and walked over to the workbench.

CHAPTER NINE

The Barricade

Jeff, Dick, and Toni stayed near the entrance to the small room of the cave. Still as statues they watched the stranger at the workbench. He was using the propane torch to melt some metal in a small iron pot. Then he took a spoon to skim off the film that had formed on the melted metal. After that he dipped out the clean metal and began pouring it into the mold.

All this while Toni had been sitting in a crouched position. Soon she felt a cramp in her leg. The pain was so great that she moved her foot to ease it, and in doing so made a faint noise. It was enough to make the stranger stare at the main entrance to the room. Not the blink of an eyelash came from the children. They sat perfectly still, the way a rabbit does when he sees an enemy. Then, as the man looked away, they relaxed once more. The shadow they were in was so dark he hadn't seen them!

After a while the children grew tired watching the stranger, and Toni decided she would much rather be home, eating a big lunch. Jeffrey and Dick had other ideas. They were wondering how to keep the man in the cave while they went to get the police. Of course, they could trail the stranger when he left the cave. Jeffrey was thinking this, but he was sure the man had a gun because he could see something bulging out of his pocket. And if the man were cornered, he would not hesitate to use the gun. A shudder ran through Jeffrey as he pictured what would happen to them, especially if the gun held more than one bullet.

Then Jeffrey leaned forward with interest. The man was hanging up a hammock that he had brought from the car. He attached it to two stones that jutted out from the wall. With a heavy sigh he climbed into the hammock, stretched himself out, and closed his eyes.

"Maybe he's gone to sleep," said Dick in a whisper after a few minutes. "Now we can go and get the police."

Jeffrey hesitated. "No. He might not really be asleep yet."

"Why don't we wait until he snores then," suggested Toni, thinking that all men snored because her father did.

In this instance Toni was right, for after a long interval the man's mouth opened wide, and loud snores filled the room.

"Come on. Let's get going," urged Dick.

"Wait. He might wake up in a little while," said Jeffrey softly. "Then we would feel stupid if we came back here with the police and he was gone. I still don't know his name or where he lives."

"You've got a point there, Jeff," whispered Dick. "We've got to figure out a way to keep him here."

"How are we going to do that?" asked Toni, wishing she could solve the problem.

Jeffrey had a plan. "Let's creep outside and plug up the entrance that he uses to get into the cave," he said. "When he wakes up, he won't be able to get out, and we can go and get the police."

"You mean we'll barricade him in here?" asked Toni.

"Sure," answered Jeff. "He won't be able to get out of the cave. That hole in the other side of this room isn't big enough for a man to crawl through. I barely got through myself. And he can't leave by the exit at Fox Hollow because the boulder is blocking the room that leads to it."

"I think your idea is swell, Jeff," said Dick. "We'd better—" He did not finish, for the man began to stir in the hammock, and he stopped snoring.

The children swallowed hard and stared at the stranger, waiting to see if he was awake. But the man's eyes remained closed, and his breathing was heavy.

"Let's go," whispered Jeff.

Very quietly the three of them hurried across the room and climbed out of the secret entrance. The sunlight felt wonderful to them but they wasted no time exclaiming over it. Instead, they sprang into action. They used the log and rock to plug up the hole. Then they gathered more rocks and piled them up until they were sure they had made a perfect barricade.

"Now I'll go and get the police," said Dick. "You had better stay here, Jeff, and keep guard."

"I'll go with you, Dick," said Toni.

Jeff bit his lip. What if the other man should come back and find him here? No doubt he would have a gun, too, Jeffrey decided. On the other hand, he knew someone had to stay. "Yes, you go and get the police," he agreed. "But don't take too long."

"You bet we won't," said Toni. And together she and Dick ran off on their important errand.

Minutes went by. They seemed like hours. Jeffrey sat on a rock, his eyes glued on the barricade. He kept listening for the sound of a car, though, and every once in awhile he looked over at the dirt road to see if one was in sight.

Finally, he heard a motor chugging in the distance. His first thought was that it was the police coming. Then he gripped his hands with fear. It might be the other man driving back!

Jeffrey did not know what to do, for to make matters worse, some of the rocks in the barricade had begun to move. The stranger had awakened. He was trying to get out.

Jeffrey jumped up and began pushing the rocks back in place. A cold sweat came over him, and he trembled from head to foot. He could not hear the car coming any more, but suddenly he heard voices —the most welcome voices in the whole world!

Dick and Toni were guiding the policeman to the barricade.

"We've really got him locked up," Toni was saying as they came into view.

After that everything happened so quickly that Jeffrey did not have a chance to speak to his friends. The policeman pushed away the barricade. Fearing that the man might be armed, he let himself down into the hole very carefully.

"There's no man down here," he said after a few minutes to the children who were peering into the entrance of the cave.

"I'll bet I know where he's gone," cried Jeff. He started to drop down into the hole.

Dick and Toni were about to follow.

"Only one of you had better come down here," said the policeman. He pointed to Jeff. "I guess it's you, son."

Jeff lowered himself into the cave and soon was leading the policeman out of the small room. They walked rapidly along the passage until the trail went in two directions. The officer was about to go to the left.

"That path takes you way into the cave," whispered Jeff. "I think he's hiding at the end of this other path. It's a dead end."

Jeffrey started to hurry along the path, but the officer motioned to him to stay behind.

Disappointed, the boy watched the policeman disappear into the darkness. He waited breathlessly to see if he was right. Sure enough, it was not long before he heard a shuffling noise. Then came the officer's voice, booming out in the stillness of the cave. "You're under arrest," he said.

"You can't arrest me," protested the stranger. "You've got nothing on me."

"That's what you think. Come on. Get going," ordered the officer, pointing a gun at the man's back.

Jeffrey waited until they reached him. The policeman looked at him and smiled. The other man leered at the boy. "So you're the smarty pants in this deal. I'll fix you!"

"No, you won't," said Jeff. "Furthermore, I want my old quarter back. It's worth fifty dollars and you took it."

"Well, well, Mr. Sands. So you've even stolen money from a boy!" exclaimed the officer. "My, you've got quite a record! Many people in this town will be surprised when they learn that their new building inspector is a counterfeiter."

Jeffrey tugged at the policeman's sleeve. "I don't understand. Is Mr. Sands a building inspector?"

"Yes. He's been working on a cleanup campaign for our city manager. He wants all the shacks torn down in this town."

Jeffrey was thinking a mile a minute, "So that's why Mr. Sands had a picture of the Explorers hut! He thought it was a shack."

The policeman replied, "I guess so, but you had better come now, son. Your friends are waiting for you outside. And I want to get this gent under lock and key."

That night there was a celebration at Jeffrey's house. His mother and father were so proud of him that they invited the neighbors for a barbecue supper in their back yard. Of course, all the neighbors came, and many others joined in the fun since all of Charlestown had heard about Jeffrey Jones, the boy who not only had saved Dick Wright's life, but had tracked down a counterfeiter.

At the party Dick's father and mother thanked Jeffrey a second time for all he had done for their son. And Jeffrey was asked to tell the guests what had happened. He suddenly became shy, though, and Dick and Toni had to take over. They told the whole story and made Jeff out quite a hero.

"Yes, he certainly is a hero," said the policeman, who had joined the group. He had stopped by to tell

Jeffrey more about Mr. Sands and to give him back his old quarter. "Your man, Jeff, is a real slick counterfeiter. We've checked on him, and he's been selling old coins to collectors all over the world. So you've done a fine job. When you're older, come around, and I'll see that you get on the police force."

Jeffrey grinned. "I will," he said. "My friends Dick and Toni helped, too, though." Then he added, "What is the date on the coin Mr. Sands was making?"

"It's a ten-dollar gold piece with the date 1858 on it," answered the officer.

"Boy! A collector would pay five thousand dollars for a ten-dollar gold piece with that date on it! I remember seeing it listed in my coin book. If it's a proof ten-dollar gold piece—that means it has a mirrorlike surface—it's worth five thousand dollars."

"You don't mean it!" exclaimed a neighbor who had been listening to the conversation.

Jeffrey nodded, and the policeman patted him on the back. "You know a lot about old coins, don't you?"

Jeffrey nodded again, and then shook hands with a newcomer to the party, a Professor Reppy from a Charlestown University.

"I showed Professor Reppy the skeleton you discovered in the cave, Jeff," said Dick.

"Is it a prehistoric animal?" asked Toni.

The professor shook his head. "No. It's the skeleton of a bear that apparently was wounded and went into the cave."

Jeffrey's face clouded with disappointment. Now he was no longer a full-fledged Explorer. He had not discovered anything unusual. Then he pricked up his ears to make sure he was hearing correctly, for the professor was still talking. "But the stone vessel and implement are very old. The vessel is called a mortar, and the tool is a pestle. They were used by the Indians many centuries ago for grinding small seeds. So you've made a remarkable discovery, Jeffrey. I would like to spend a day with you and your friends in the cave and see if we can't find more material."

"Golly! We'll be real spelunkers!" exclaimed Toni, delighted that she had remembered the other name for cave crawlers.

"Boy, what fun that will be!" cried Dick. "We might discover some other secret rooms in the cave. We've got to have a conference on this right away, Jeff, at the Explorers hut."

"Oh, jeepers," said Jeffrey, "I forgot to tell you about the Explorers hut. It's going to be torn down."

"Torn down!" cried the Explorers.

"Yes," answered Jeff. He told about the town cleanup campaign, put on by the city manager. "So we've got to ask him not to tear it down," finished Jeffrey.

"That will not be necessary," said Dick's father. "All the neighbors on our street have decided they want to keep the hut for you Explorers. The manager agreed."

"Hurrah!" cried the Explorers.

Then Dick turned to Jeffrey. "Come on, Jeff. You're our top Explorer. Let's head for the hut right away."

www.ingramcontent.com/pod-product-compliance
Lightning Source LLC
Chambersburg PA
CBHW020412150626
46554CB00013B/828